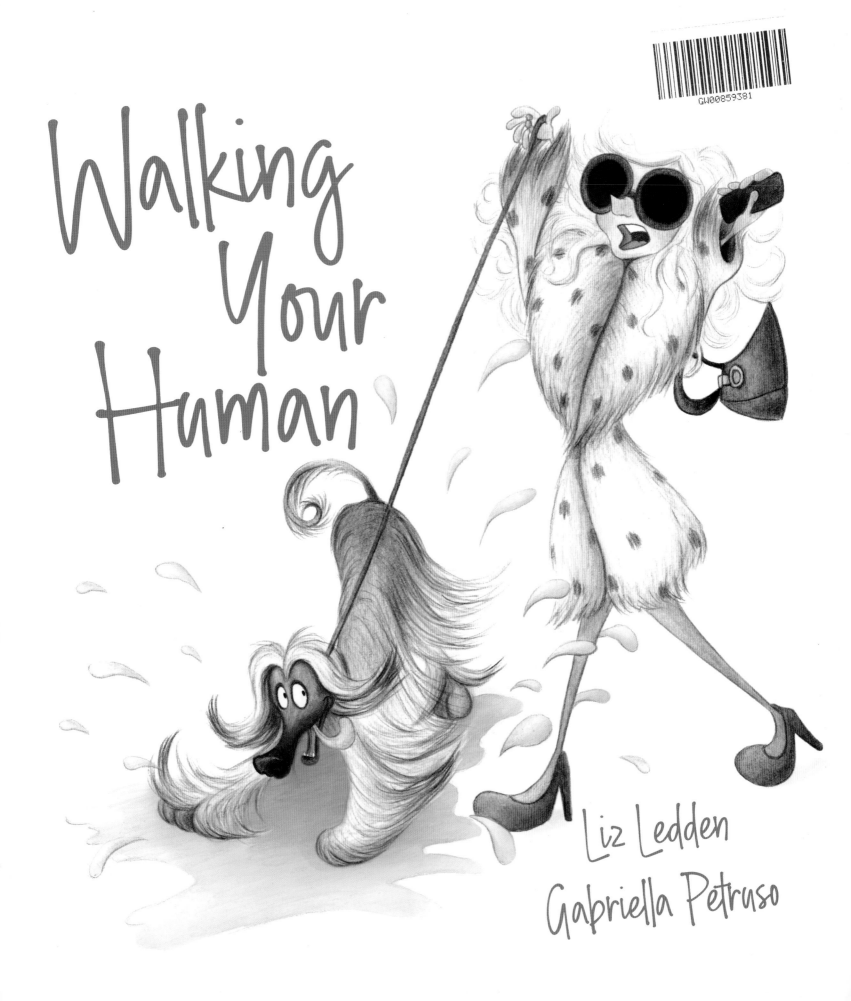

Walking Your Human

Liz Ledden

Gabriella Petruso

If you ever see your human relaxing, don't be fooled.

They're waiting to be walked.

Sometimes...

...they'll need a bit of encouragement.

And don't forget to **surprise** them.

Humans **love** surprises.

They also **love** to run.

It's good for them.

Don't forget to
stop
for a
drink...

...and let them explore too.

Sometimes, your human

will need protecting.

They'll **always** be grateful.

When your human gets distracted...

...be sure to keep them moving.

And it's

important

that they don't

overheat.

Let them see your talents,

like **fetching**, **digging** and **burying**.

If you see a camera,
strike a pose!

It's all about making memories.

Stop to show them **a beautiful view...**

...and if you're lucky enough to get a present,

be sure to share.

When it's time to head home, *be firm with your human.*

Sometimes, they don't know when **enough** is **enough**.

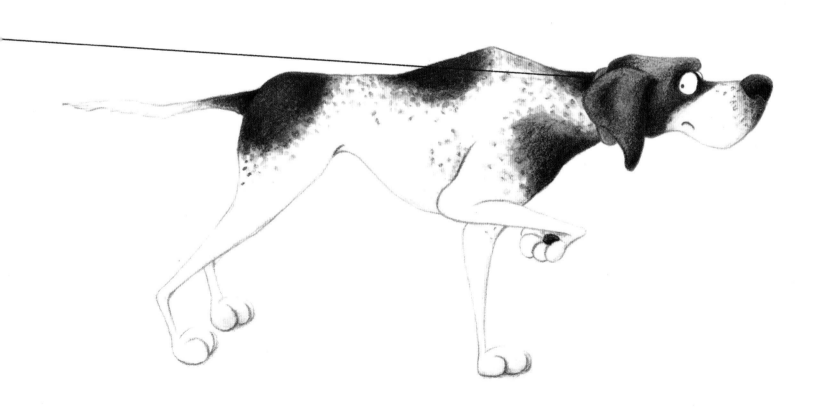

After the walk, your human might play
hide and seek.

When you find them,

make sure they don't run away.

Teach your human how to **properly relax**.

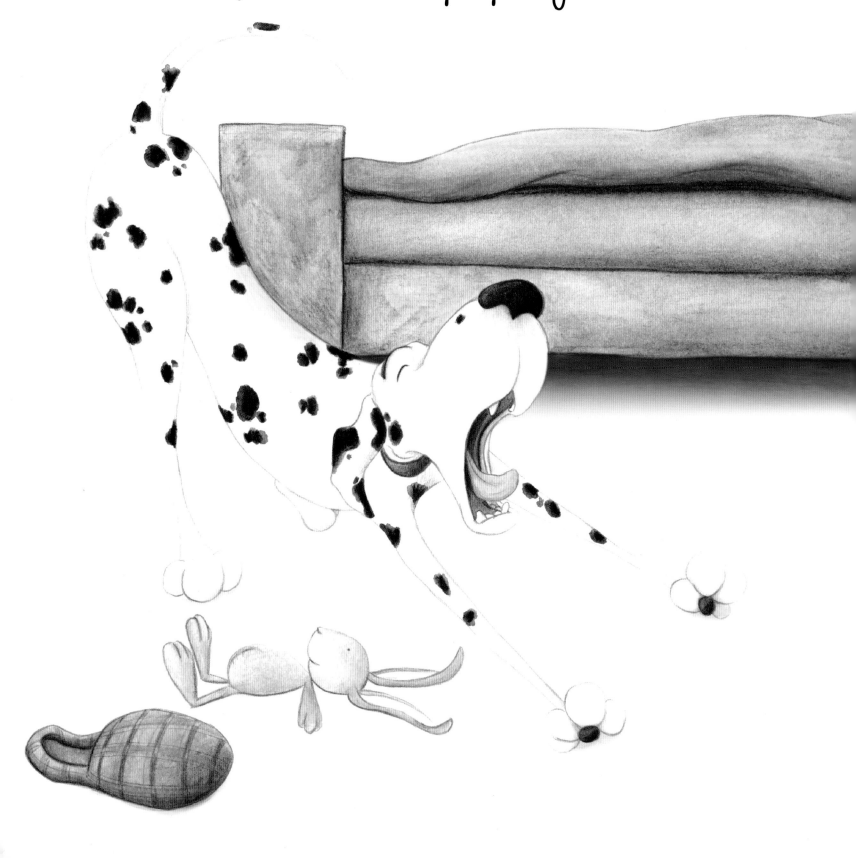

You can't walk them **all** the time.

Liz Ledden

Liz Ledden has long escaped between the pages of a good book, and was a 'reading by torchlight under the covers' kind of child. She now turns a blind eye to her own kids doing the same.

Liz co-hosts kids' book podcast One More Page, and has written in various formats for companies and publications. She's lived in Vietnam, Cambodia and Canada, has a rescue dog named Frankie who acts like a cat, and can typically be found maxing out her library card.

Gabriella Petruso

Gabriella lives in the UK with her daft dog, partner and son. She's lucky to live within cycling distance of a zoo, where she and her sketchbook can be spotted in their natural habitat. Using coloured ink and pencil she creates humorous characters - the hairier and more unconventional the better!

After originally training in medicine, Gabriella won an award for her artwork in 2017 and has been thoroughly enjoying pursuing her love of picture books since. Walking Your Human is Gabriella's 2nd book and she is excited to bring more of her loveable characters to the page!

Larrikin House

An imprint of Learning Discovery Pty Ltd
142-144 Frankston Dandenong Rd, Dandenong South Victoria 3175 Australia

www.larrikinhouse.com

First Published in Australia by Larrikin House 2021 (larrikinhouse.com)

Written by: Liz Ledden
Illustrated by: Gabriella Petruso

Cover Designed by: Mary Anastasiou
Design & Artwork by: Mary Anastasiou (imaginecreative.com.au)

A CIP catalogue record for this book is available from the National Library of Australia. http://catalogue.nla.gov.au

ISBN: 9780648894513 (Hardback)
ISBN: 9780648894520 (Paperback)
ISBN: 9780648894537 (Big Book)

FORESTFRIENDLY
This book is printed on paper sourced from sustainable forests

NATIONAL LIBRARY OF AUSTRALIA

A catalogue record for this book is available from the National Library of Australia